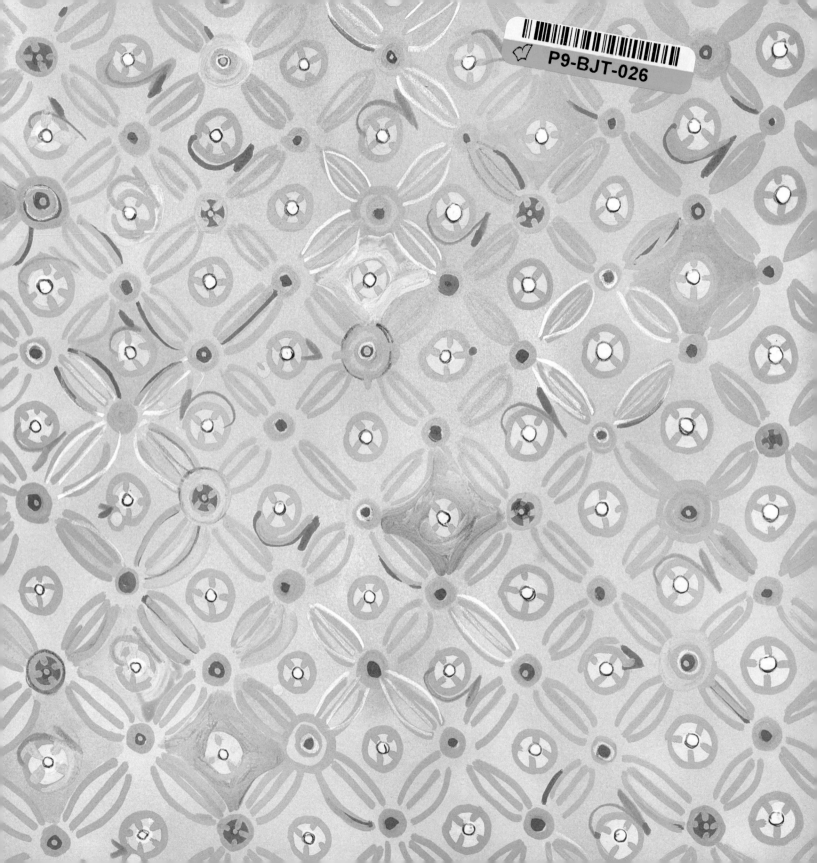

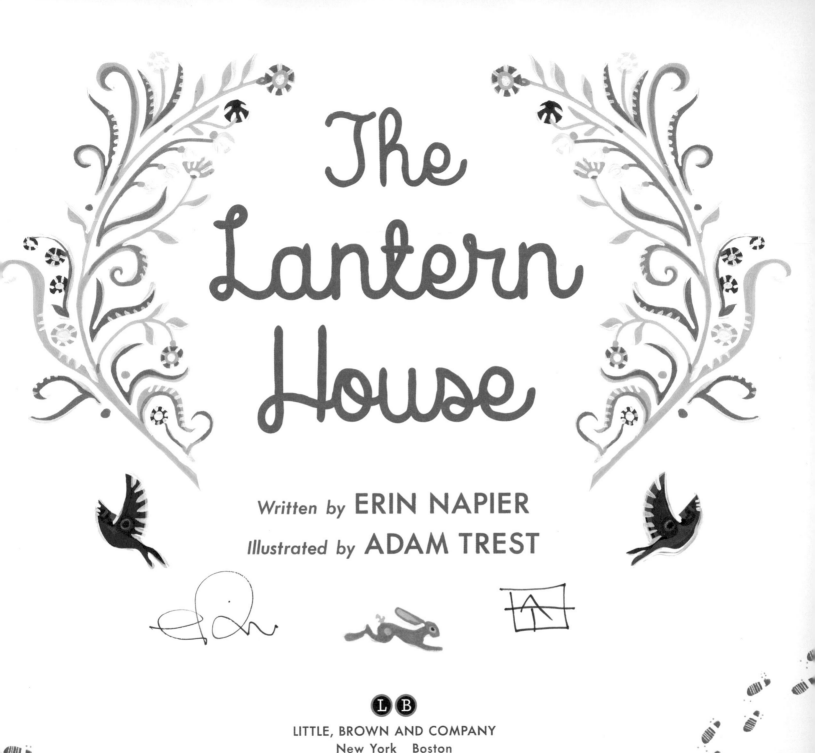

The Lantern House

Written by **ERIN NAPIER**

Illustrated by **ADAM TREST**

LB

LITTLE, BROWN AND COMPANY
New York   Boston

ABOUT THIS BOOK
The illustrations for this book were done in
acrylic ink and acrylic gouache on 100% cotton paper. This book was
edited by Andrea Spooner and designed by Patrick Collins with art direction
from Saho Fujii. The production was supervised by Ruiko Tokunaga, and the production
editor was Jen Graham. The text was set in Payson WF, and the display type is Catalina Script.

Little, Brown and Company • Hachette Book Group • 1290 Avenue of the Americas, New York, NY 10104 Visit us at LBYR.com • First Edition: May 2022 • Little, Brown and Company is a division of Hachette Book Group, Inc. • The Little, Brown name and logo are trademarks of Hachette Book Group, Inc. • The publisher is not responsible for websites (or their content) that are not owned by the publisher. • Library of Congress Cataloging-in-Publication Data • Names: Napier, Erin, author. | Trest, Adam, illustrator. • Title: The lantern house / Erin Napier ; illustrated by Adam Trest. • Description: First edition. | New York : Little, Brown and Company, 2022. | Audience: Ages 4-8. | Summary: Over multiple generations, different families make changes to a house in order to make it a home. • Identifiers: LCCN 2021027566 | ISBN 9780316379601 (hardcover) | ISBN 9780316463836 (ebook) • Subjects: CYAC: Home-Fiction. | Dwellings-Fiction. | Families-Fiction. | LCGFT: Picture books. • Classification: LCC PZ7.1.N3626 Lan 2022 | DDC [E]-dc23 • LC record available at https://lccn.loc.gov/2021027566 • ISBNs: 978-0-316-37960-1 (hardcover), 978-0-316-46383-6 (ebook), 978-0-316-46403-1 (ebook), 978-0-316-46413-0 (ebook) • PRINTED IN THE USA • PHX • 10 9 8 7 6 5 4 3 2 1

For Helen and Mae
—EN

For Cyndi
—AT

I am a brand-new house,
and I glow like a lantern
in the night. I will keep a
family safe from the storms
and warm in the winter.
I will be home.

A couple builds a picket fence around
my feet and plants flowers in my yard.
    They paint one room
green, and I watch them
waiting and waiting.

One day they bring home a wriggling,
wrinkly baby girl.

She learns to play the piano
in my living room

and chases the dog
in my backyard.

I watch her grow with the pencil marks on the laundry room doorway and miss her when she goes to school.

She meets a boy, who sits with her on my
porch and holds her hand while my swing sways
them in the summer wind.

One day she marries that boy at my fireplace hearth and moves away to a house of her own.

The couple is older now. Sometimes the two
of them eat dinner on my back porch and
dance to the radio in my dining room,

but the days are growing quieter,
and the nights are calm and sleepy.

The girl is a mama now and brings her little boy to visit his grandparents, where they teach him how to plant tomatoes and climb the magnolia tree, and how to make biscuits in the old cast-iron skillet.

My glow is dimmer than
it used to be, with only one
bedside lamp on in the night.
My blue paint is fading, and the
picket fence is broken in places,
but the woman still carefully,
slowly sweeps away the fallen
leaves. She eats alone now, but
I keep her company and hold
her close in the storms.

One night the lamp does not come on, and my windows stay dark. The mailbox is empty. Only the leaves dance now, in the corners of my porch, and the spiders spin their webs where the girl once slept. Dust collects where the piano once sat. I creak in the winter wind.

Sometimes I dream about a family who will love me again.

Will I take care of a painter?

Or a trapeze artist?

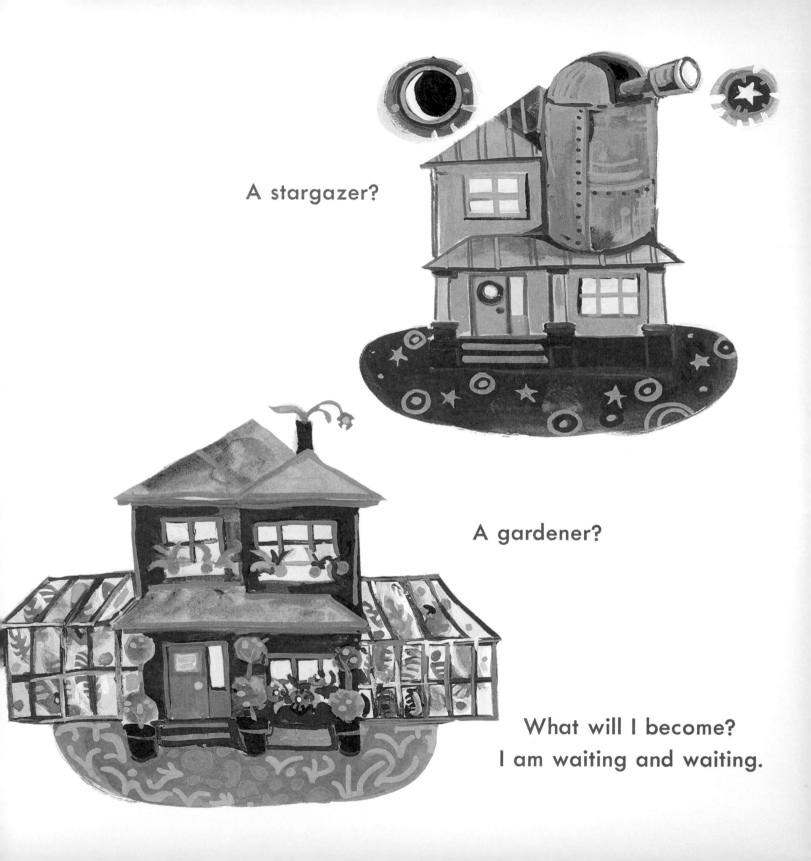

A stargazer?

A gardener?

What will I become?
I am waiting and waiting.

One day my front door opens and
a family steps quietly inside, a little
boy hiding behind his parents' legs.
"This could be home," they say.

They are not afraid of my spiders
and broken parts. Though I am dark
and empty, they stay with me.

They paint me yellow and plant roses along
my new picket fence.

They wallpaper my halls and sweep the spiderwebs away.

After my family cooks dinner in my kitchen,
the father plays guitar and they dance.
Even though I am old, I can dance too as
my floors creak along.

When dusk falls, there is light in every room, and I glow like a lantern in the night. Smoke rises from my chimney. I am waiting and waiting for the golden sun to wake my family so we can begin another day together.

Though I am a very old house, a family is beginning a brand-new story here. I will keep them safe from the storms and warm in the winter.

I am home.